Humphrey'
Christm

CW00792697

Humphrey's Christmas Fun

Betty G. Birney worked at Disneyland and the Disney Studios, has written many children's television shows and is the author of over forty books, including the bestselling *The World According to Humphrey*, which won the Richard and Judy Children's Book Club Award, *Friendship According to Humphrey, Trouble According to Humphrey, Surprises According to Humphrey, More Adventures According to Humphrey, Holidays According to Humphrey, School According to Humphrey, Mysteries According to Humphrey* and *Christmas According to Humphrey*, and seven books in the Humphrey's Tiny Tales series. Her work has won many awards, including an Emmy and three Humanitas Prizes. She lives in America with her husband.

Humphrey's Book of Christmas Fun

Betty G. Birney

Compiled by Amanda Li

faber and faber

First published in 2013
by Faber and Faber Limited
Bloomsbury House, 74-77 Great Russell Street
London WC1B 3DA

Printed and bound by
CPI Group (UK) Ltd, Croydon, CR0 4YY

Graphic design by Patrick Tate

A CIP record for this book
is available from the British Library

978–0–571–28241–8

2 4 6 8 10 9 7 5 3 1

Santa's Sack

Do you feel excited on Christmas Eve because Santa is coming? I know exactly how you feel – I get so excited when Ms Mac is due for a visit that I can barely squeak!

Would you like to know one of the presents that Santa is bringing in his sack? Then cross out all the letters that appear twice. Rearrange the remaining letters to find out what the present is.

Festive Word Grid

Just about everything to do with Christmas is **FUN-FUN-FUN!** This word grid contains so many great things about Christmas.

If you guess the correct answers going across the word grid, you will find something I enjoy listening to in the vertical box

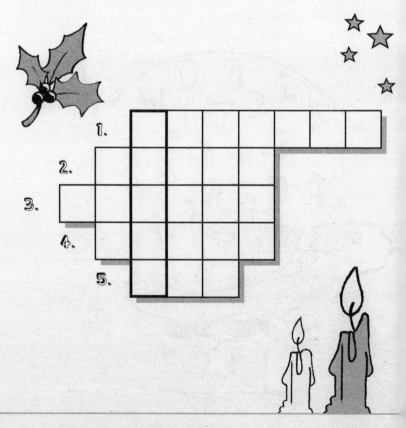

1.

2.

3.

4.

5.

1. People like to light these at Christmas time. They look beautiful!

2. You can't wrap a present without this (and sticky tape, too).

3. A Christmas dinner favourite – with stuffing and cranberry sauce.

4. A plant with red berries – be careful of the prickly leaves!

5. A special Christmas cake. It is shaped like a Yule _ _ _ .

Humphrey's Jolly Jokes 1

What do ducks love about Christmas?
Pulling the Christmas quackers.

> Animals love Christmas, too. Maybe this year I'll send my rodent friends 'Chris-mouse' cards!

Who brings Christmas presents for dogs?
Santa Paws.

Which deer has the worst table manners?
Rude-olph.

What hangs from the ceiling at Christmas and says 'Ribbet ribbet'??
The mistle-toad!

What do skunks sing at Christmas?
'Jingle smells, jingle smells . . .'

Christmas Wordsearch

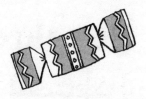

JOY-JOY-JOY! Christmas is the season of good will. And what I love about this time of year is that everyone is so happy. I like it when there's something to celebrate!

This wordsearch contains eight festive words. Can you find them? They may be up, down, across or diagonal.

CRACKER · CAROL · ADVENT · GAMES
PRESENTS · PARTY · SANTA CLAUS · TINSEL

S	E	H	G	L	O	R	A	C
A	C	G	A	I	K	I	H	R
N	K	A	M	C	H	T	R	A
T	S	O	E	L	N	I	A	C
A	O	H	S	E	L	L	N	K
C	K	V	V	P	E	S	A	E
L	S	D	I	S	A	E	N	R
A	A	R	N	L	B	R	W	C
U	N	I	G	B	A	V	T	G
S	T	N	E	S	E	R	P	Y

Humphrey Sings

I like hearing carol singers coming to the house. I can squeak along with them and get into the Christmas spirit!

How many Christmas carols do you know? Can you fill in the missing words from these song titles?

1. Silent _____

2. Away in a _____

3. The _____ Noel

4. The _____ Days of Christmas

5. Hark the Herald _____ Sing

6. Deck the _____

7. Good _____ Wenceslas

8. O Little _____ of Bethlehem

squeak!

squeak!

Halls	Twelve	Angels	First
Town	Night	Manger	King

Design a Christmas Sweater

The teachers at Longfellow School often dress up at Christmas. Mr Morales always wears a snazzy Christmas tie and, one year, Mrs Brisbane wore a red-and-green striped sweater and a Santa hat – I pawsitively loved them!

Can you design a Christmas sweater for your favourite teacher to wear?

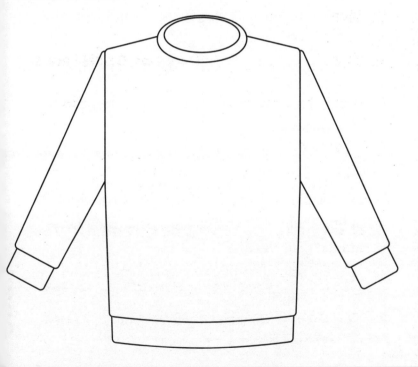

Aldo's Christmas Ladder

My good friend Aldo is always **BUSY-BUSY-BUSY** at Christmas time! There are decorations to hang, trees to put up, parties to arrange – he's such a helpful person.

This year, I know he'd really like a bike to get around the town more easily. Can you help me put a shiny new bike for Aldo into Santa's sack?

To complete the puzzle, read the clues and write the answer in the space. But you can only change ONE letter from the previous word – starting with BIKE.

1. This is a man's name. It is also a short word for 'microphone'.
2. It would be a really long way for me to run! But most humans can walk this distance.
3. Lots of the students from Room 26 like to drink this at break time – it leaves a funny white moustache around their mouths!
4. A lovely, soft fabric that's nice to touch. I wish I had some to snuggle up in!
5. This is what I would be if you gave me chocolate to eat – it's not good for a hamster!

BIKE

1. _ _ _ _
2. _ _ _ _
3. _ _ _ _
4. _ _ _ _
5. _ _ _ _
6. _ _ _ _
7. _ _ _ _
8. _ _ _ _

SACK

6. What you would do to a lollipop. (I would rather do this to a piece of apple.)
7. My cage door has one of these, but it doesn't close properly and I can get out when no one's around!
8. Something humans wear on their feet (underneath their shoes).

Finish the Elf

I've noticed that when everyone in Room 26 works together as a team, a lot gets done.

Santa Claus needs many helpers to get his job done. And getting all those gifts delivered on time is a real team effort!

Can you finish drawing this picture of one of Santa's helpful elves?

Festive Sudoku 1

Sudoku is a great puzzle that comes from Japan – where Mrs Brisbane's son, Jason, lives!

To complete the puzzle you must fill in the spaces with a picture of a Christmas pudding, a sprig of holly, a Christmas tree or a bauble. But there's an important Sudoku rule – each of the four Christmas objects must appear only once in each row (going across) and once in each column (going down).

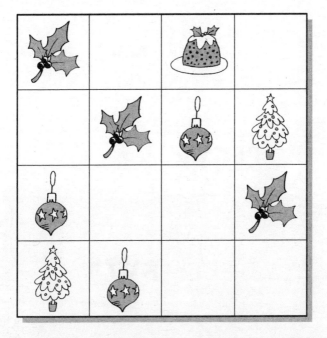

Santa Around the World

I'll never know how Santa gets around the world in **ONE-ONE-ONE** night to visit all the children. But somehow he does!

On the luggage tags below are just six of the many countries that Santa visits on his travels. But they're all mixed up. Can you unscramble them?

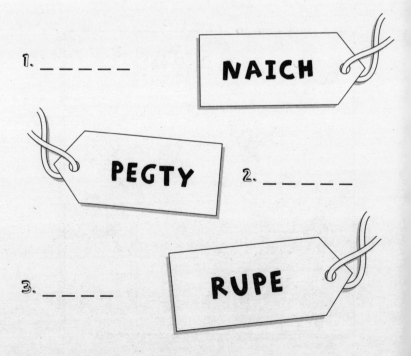

1. _ _ _ _ _

NAICH

PEGTY

2. _ _ _ _ _

3. _ _ _ _

RUPE

4. _ _ _ _ _   **DAINI**

YILAT   5. _ _ _ _ _

6. _ _ _ _ _ _   **DANACA**

Twelve Day Twirl

'On the first day of Christmas, my true love gave to me…'

Oh, I love to sing – though it might sound like very faint squeaking to you!

Can you find all the creatures and characters from this famous song? Look at this twirling word spiral – some words will be going forwards, others backwards. Cross each one out with a pencil as you find it.

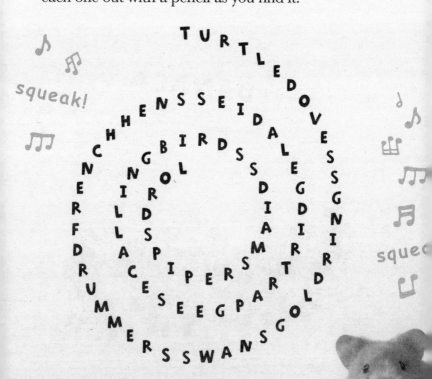

Decorate the Tree

One of the most fun parts of getting ready for Christmas is helping to decorate the tree. Then I can gaze at the **SHINY-SHINY-SHINY** baubles, lights and stars from my cage – beautiful!

Can you decorate this Christmas tree? Don't forget to put a fairy or a star at the top!

Humphrey's Jolly Jokes 2

What do snowmen eat for breakfast?
Snowflakes.

There's 'snow' joke like a snowman joke!

What do you get if you cross a snowman with a vampire?
Frostbite.

What do you call a party for snowmen?
A snowball.

What goes 'Now you see me, now you don't, now you see me, now you don't'?
A snowman on a zebra crossing.

What do you call a snowman in July?
A puddle.

Snowy True or False?

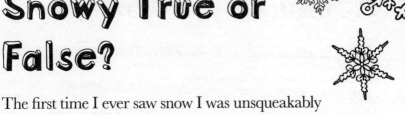

The first time I ever saw snow I was unsqueakably surprised! It looked so soft and beautiful falling from the sky – but actually, it was COLD and WET!

I know a lot more about snow now – how about you? Do you know if these snow facts are true or false?

		TRUE	FALSE
1.	Every snowflake has six sides.	☐	☐
2.	All snowflakes are identical.	☐	☐
3.	About 12 per cent of the Earth's surface is covered in permanent snow and ice.	☐	☐
4.	Snow forms in clouds where the temperature is below freezing	☐	☐
5.	Light and fluffy snow is often called 'powder'.	☐	☐
6.	Snow is made out of tiny ice crystals.	☐	☐
7.	A really severe snowstorm is called a tornado.	☐	☐
8.	Snow is white.	☐	☐

Humphrey's Tip: Number 8 is a tricky one! Don't go for the obvious answer.

Finish the Snowman

Building a snowman is **FUN-FUN-FUN**! Especially putting on a carrot for a nose!

Can you complete this snowman? He needs a happy face, a hat and a scarf, some buttons and twig arms.

Snowman Spot-the-difference

Snow is great stuff – but too cold for me! I love watching out of the window when the children are building snowmen. Today they've made six of them – but just one is different. Can you tell which one?

A

B

C

D

E

F

Humphrey's Secret Christmas Code

A   J   S

B   K   T

C   L   U

D   M   V

E   N   W

F   O   X

G   P   Y

H   Q   Z

I   R

I just love secret codes! In my little notebook I've been making up a **GREAT-GREAT-GREAT** Christmas code just for you.

Now I've written you a special Christmas message. Do you want to find out what it is? Then look at the picture code opposite and write each letter in the space below.

___ ___ ___ ___ ___ ___ ___ ___ ___ ___

___ ___ ___ ___ ___ ___ ___ ___

___ ___ ___ ___ ___ ___

Christmas Humphrey Dot-to-dot

Join the dots to see one of my favourite festive objects – it's right behind me!

Reindeer Wordsearch

Santa's reindeer work very hard to deliver all the presents on Christmas Eve. So make sure you leave a delicious crunchy carrot out for them as a treat!

This wordsearch contains the names of Santa's nine reindeer. Can you find them? They may be up, down, across or diagonal.

**RUDOLPH · DASHER · DANCER · PRANCER · VIXEN
COMET · CUPID · DONNER · BLITZEN**

P	R	A	N	C	E	R	N	C
A	C	G	A	I	U	I	H	R
R	E	N	N	O	D	P	R	A
B	S	H	E	L	N	I	I	T
L	D	H	P	E	L	N	E	D
I	K	A	V	L	E	M	A	A
T	S	D	N	M	O	E	N	S
Z	A	R	F	C	B	D	W	H
E	N	O	G	B	E	V	U	E
N	E	X	I	V	E	R	P	R

Tasty Wordsnake

My friends tell me that Christmas food is so **TASTY-TASTY-TASTY**! Personally, I love to nibble on the oranges, raisins and nuts that are always around at Christmas time.

Can you find all these yummy Yuletide treats in the wordsnake opposite? Use a pencil to draw a continuous line through the words, which are in the same order as the list below. The line will snake up and down, backwards and forward – but never diagonally.

PUDDING
PIE
CAKE
TURKEY
GRAVY
SAUCE
SPROUT
CANDY
ORANGE
STUFFING
CREAM

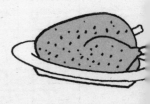

P	U	N	D	A	M
D	D	A	Y	E	R
I	N	C	O	G	C
P	G	T	R	N	I
I	E	U	A	N	F
A	C	O	R	G	F
K	E	S	P	E	U
U	T	E	C	S	T
R	Y	G	U	A	S
K	E	R	A	V	Y

Humphrey's Jolly Jokes 3

There's so much food around at Christmas that everyone's like a turkey — stuffed!

What are brown and creep around the kitchen?

Mince spies.

What's the best thing to put into a turkey?

Your teeth.

What do snowmen put on their Christmas dinner?

Chilli sauce.

How does Good King Wenceslas like his pizza?

Deep pan, crisp and even.

Knock, knock.

Who's there?

Police.

Police who?

Police don't make me eat Brussel sprouts!

Save them for me — I just love Brussel sprouts!

Delicious Dot-to-dot

Mmm! Something smells unsqueakably **GOOD-GOOD-GOOD**! Join the dots to find out what it is.

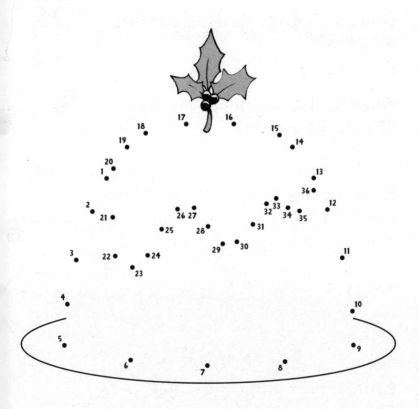

Snowflake Sorting

Ms Lark, the music teacher, organised a wonderful winter show at Longfellow School. Some of the class dressed up as glittering snowflakes and whirled around the stage – they looked so beautiful!

Take a look at this snowflake puzzle. Like real life, all the snowflakes are slightly different. But one has been repeated – can you find the matching pair?

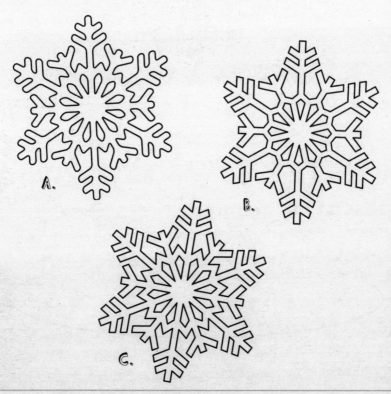

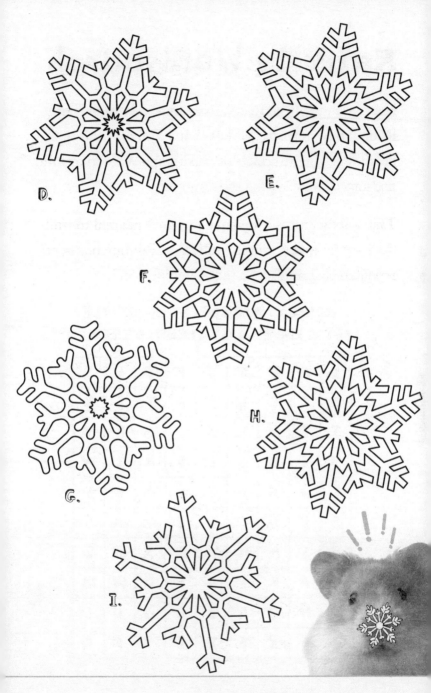

D.

E.

F.

G.

H.

I.

Nativity Wordsearch

Have you ever been in a nativity play? My friends in Room 26 performed one last year – Garth was Joseph, Heidi was Mary and lots of children played donkeys and sheep!

This wordsearch contains seven words related to the Nativity. Can you find them? They may be up, down, across or diagonal.

**DONKEY · MANGER · STAR · STABLE
BETHLEHEM · BABY JESUS · WISE MEN**

B	A	B	Y	J	E	S	U	S
E	C	E	L	B	A	T	S	R
T	E	N	Y	O	D	A	R	A
H	S	H	E	L	R	R	I	W
L	D	H	P	E	L	N	E	I
E	K	O	G	L	E	M	A	S
H	S	N	N	M	O	X	N	E
E	A	R	F	K	B	D	W	M
M	N	O	G	B	E	G	U	E
Q	E	X	F	V	E	Y	P	N

Festive Sudoku 2

Sudoku is a great puzzle that comes from Japan – just like my cute little hamster toy, Rockin' Aki!

To complete the puzzle you must fill in the spaces with a picture of a Christmas pudding, sprig of holly, Christmas tree or bauble. But there's an important Sudoku rule – each of the four Christmas objects must appear only once in each row (going across) and once in each column (going down).

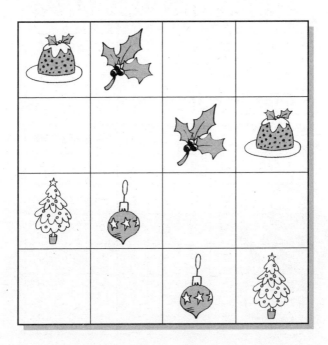

Rockin' Rhymes

Writing poems and rhymes is **FUN-FUN-FUN**! And what could be more fun to write about than Christmas!

> **With gifts and tasty things to eat**
> **Christmas time is such a _ _ _ _ _ !**

> **It's really fun for us to play**
> **A family game on Christmas _ _ _ .**

> **Coat, hat, gloves and out we go**
> **Into the cold, white, crunchy _ _ _ _ .**

What's Santa carrying on his back?
It's full of presents, it's a _ _ _ _ !

When Santa comes, he's out of sight,
He's very quiet and comes at _ _ _ _ _.

Hang your stockings up with care
And in the morning,
see what's _ _ _ _ _!

Odd One Out

Take a close look at all these Christmas items.

Can you circle one picture in each set of three that is the odd one out?

1.

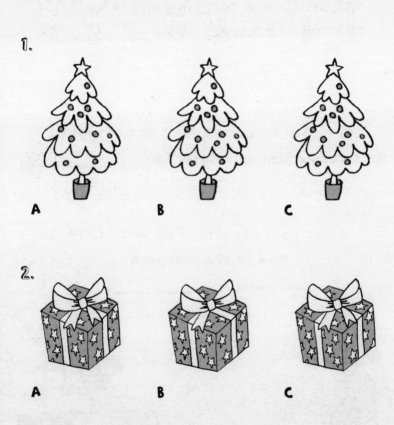

A   B   C

2.

A   B   C

3.

A   B   C

4.

A   B   C

ho ho ho !!!

Humphrey's Jolly Jokes 4

What do you get if you cross Father Christmas with a detective?

Santa Clues.

You call him Santa Claus — we rodents know him as Santa Claws! Here are my all-time favourite Santa jokes.

What do Santa's elves learn at school?

The elf-abet.

What does Santa Claus write on his Christmas cards?

ABCDEFGHIJK_MNOPQRSTUVWXYZ. (NO-L!)

What did Mrs Claus say to Santa Claus?

'It looks like rain, dear.'

Why does Santa like gardening so much?

He likes to hoe, hoe, hoe!

Design a Christmas Card

When lovely Ms Mac (sigh!) came back from Brazil, she brought everyone Christmas cards from her Brazilian students. They were **PRETTY-PRETTY-PRETTY**.

Would you like to design a Christmas card to send to someone in another country? Draw your design here:

Santa's Wordsnake

Wouldn't it be unsqueakably fun to run around Santa's workshop and watch everything that's going on?

Find lots of things that are important to Santa Claus in the wordsnake opposite. Use a pencil to draw a continuous line through the words, which are in the same order as the list below. The line will snake up and down, backwards and forward – but never diagonally.

SANTA

WORKSHOP

SACK

PRESENT

SLEIGH

REINDEER

ELF

CHIMNEY

BELL

SNOW

TREE

START ⇨

S	A	S	E	E	E
T	N	E	N	R	T
A	W	R	T	O	W
R	O	P	S	N	S
K	C	K	L	L	L
S	A	I	E	E	B
H	S	G	H	E	Y
O	P	E	R	N	M
D	N	I	L	F	I
E	E	R	E	C	H

Reindeer True or False?

We all know that reindeer do a great job of pulling Santa's sleigh. But how much more do you know about them?

Try this quick quiz and tick 'True' or 'False'. Or just take a guess!

TRUE FALSE

1. Another word for reindeer is caribou. ☐ ☐
2. Reindeer are good swimmers. ☐ ☐
3. Only male reindeer have antlers. ☐ ☐
4. Male reindeers have a very loud call. ☐ ☐
5. Reindeer can lower the temperature in their legs – this helps conserve their body heat. ☐ ☐
6. Reindeer can only move slowly. ☐ ☐
7. In winter, reindeer grow long hair to protect their muzzles from the snow. ☐ ☐
8. In the song, Rudolph the reindeer was famous for his very shiny antlers. ☐ ☐

Finish the Reindeer

Oh deer! This poor reindeer is missing his antlers.

Can you draw some for him? That will really cheer
him up!

Rudolph's Dot-to-dot

Do you have any 'i-deer' what this dot-to-dot might be?
I'm guessing you might do – so let's find out!

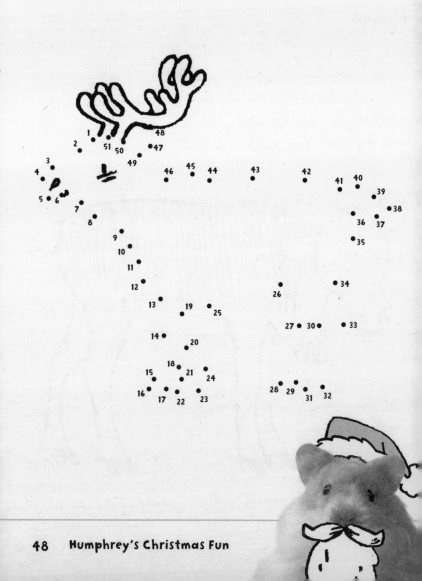

Humphrey Sings 2

I love to squeak along to all the tuneful Christmas songs – how about you?

Can you fill in the missing words to these well known songs?

1. I'm Dreaming of a _ _ _ _ _ _ Christmas.

2. Walking in a _ _ _ _ _ _ _ Wonderland

3. When a _ _ _ _ _ _ is Born

4. _ _ _ _ _ _ _ _ the Red-nosed Reindeer

5. _ _ _ _ _ _ _ the Snowman

6. We Wish You a _ _ _ _ _ _ Christmas

7. _ _ _ _ _ _ _ _ _ _ _ _ is Comin' to Town

8. _ _ _ _ _ _ _ Bells

squeak!

squeak!

Festive Food

I can't wait to crunch on all the Christmas vegetables – especially the carrots!

Can you match up the pairs of words to make some delicious Christmas foods?

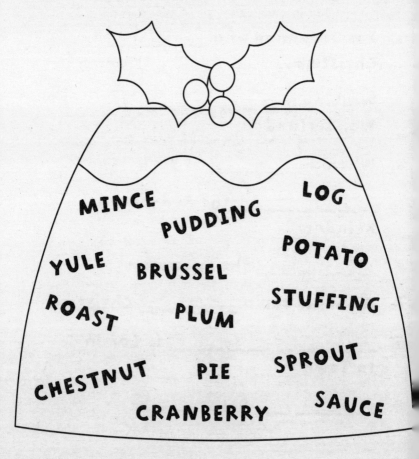

MINCE

PUDDING

LOG

YULE

BRUSSEL

POTATO

ROAST

PLUM

STUFFING

CHESTNUT

PIE

SPROUT

CRANBERRY

SAUCE

Humphrey's Tasty Treat

yum yum!

CRUNCH-CRUNCH-CRUNCH! I took a little bite out of a Christmas tree decoration. Oh my! It was delicious!

Discover what it was made out of by crossing out alternate letters on this decoration, in a clockwise direction, starting with the circled A. The remaining letters will spell out something tasty!

— — — — — — — — — — —

Write the word here

Mistletoe Mix-up

It's traditional to hang mistletoe from the ceiling and kiss someone you love underneath it. I saw Mr and Mrs Brisbane doing that last Christmas – they looked very **HAPPY-HAPPY-HAPPY**!

How many words can you make from the word MISTLETOE?

....

....

....

....

....

....

....

....

....

Humphrey's Jolly Jokes 5

What's invisible but smells like milk and cookies?

Santa's burps!

I've just realised that there's one thing you get in December that you don't get in any other month — the letter 'D'!

What do elves write on their Christmas cards?

'Wishing you a fairy merry Christma

What did the Christmas tree say to the baubles?

'Aren't you tired of hanging around?'

How do you scare a snowman?

Get a hairdryer out!

How do you drain Brussel sprouts?

With an advent colander.

Humphrey's Secret Christmas Code 2

A

B

C

D

E

F

G

H

I

J

K

L

M

N

O

P

Q

R

S

T

U

V

W

X

Y

Z

I think you'll agree that secret codes are fun to solve. They're fun to make up too – so here's another one for you!

To discover my message, look at the picture code opposite and write each letter in the space below.

____ _____

_____ _____

_____

__ __ __ __ __ __ __ __ __ ?

Humphrey's Christmas List

Giving gifts makes you feel **GOOD-GOOD-GOOD**! I once made Og the frog a Christmas tree out of Froggy Food Sticks – his '**BOING BOING BOING**!' showed me how much he appreciated it!

If I could I'd like to give everyone a Christmas present. Here are some of my ideas. Can you fill in the missing letters? They are all vowels – A, E, I, O or U.

For Mrs Brisbane — some relaxing b_bbl_ b_th

For Mr Morales — a fun Christmas t_e

For Aldo — a new br _ _ m

For 'Do-it-now' Daniel - a new story b _ _ k

For Forgetful Phoebe — a di__ry to write everything down in

For Mrs Wright — a quieter wh__stl_

For Ms Lark — some new p_ _ no music

Finish the Gift

It's so exciting to see all the presents under the tree and wonder what could be inside them! And even better to see all my friends' faces when they open their gifts on Christmas Day. I can't **WAIT-WAIT-WAIT**!

Take a look at this surprise gift. Can you finish drawing the other half? Then decorate it with a lovely pattern.

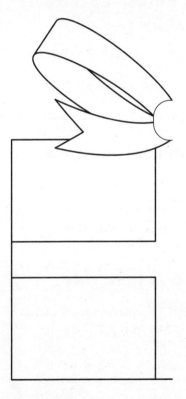

Rockin' Rhymes 2

I think you'll recognise some of these rhymes – they are all from Christmas songs and poems that I **LOVE-LOVE-LOVE** to hear!

Can you remember the rhyming words and fill them in?

**'Twas the night before Christmas
When all through the house
Not a creature was stirring,
Not even a _____ .**

**Away in a manger, no crib for a bed,
The little Lord Jesus lay down
His sweet _____ .**

**Jingle bells, jingle bells,
Jingle all the way,
Oh what fun it is to ride
On a one-horse open _____ .**

Rudolph the red-nosed reindeer
Had a very shiny nose
And if you ever saw him
You would even say it _____.

Deck the halls with boughs of holly,
'Tis the season to be _____.

And then, in a twinkling,
I heard on the roof
The prancing and pawing
Of each little _____.

Silent night, holy night
All is calm, all is _____.

Hark the Herald Angels sing!
Glory to the new born _____.

What's in the Tree?

Do you want to know who is sitting in the Christmas tree? Then cross out all the letters that appear twice. Rearrange the letters that are left to find the answer.

Christmas Tree Maze

Every Christmas tree needs something special at the top.
I like to see a shining star, an angel or a glittery fairy!

This little fairy needs to get up to the top of her tree –
can you help her find her way?

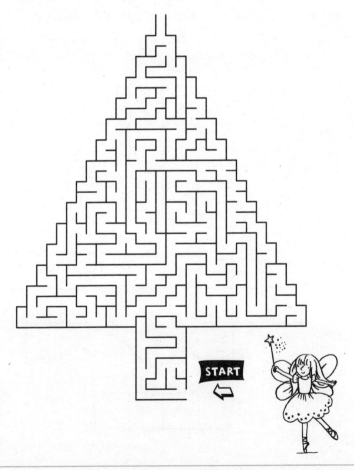

Christmas Picture Crossword

Just thinking about Christmas fills me with **JOY-JOY-JOY!**

Look at the Christmas pictures opposite. Can you complete the crossword grid with their names?

Humphrey's Tip:
Make sure you
count the letters
and spaces
carefully before
you write in
the words!

PROPERTY
OF SANTA:
DO NOT OPEN!

Panto Puzzler

Have you ever heard of a pantomime? It's a traditional Christmas show based on a fairy story, with lots of singing and jokes. It sounds like a lot of **FUN-FUN-FUN**!

Here are some famous 'pantos' and some of the characters and objects that feature in them. Can you match them up?

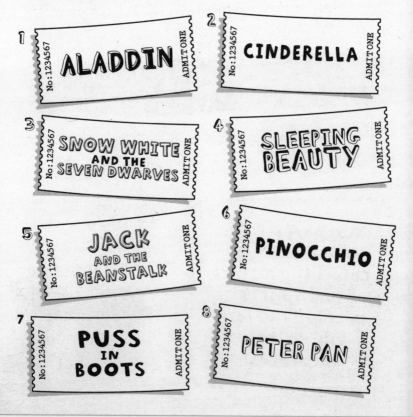

1. No: 1234567 — **ALADDIN** — ADMIT ONE
2. No: 1234567 — **CINDERELLA** — ADMIT ONE
3. No: 1234567 — **SNOW WHITE AND THE SEVEN DWARVES** — ADMIT ONE
4. No: 1234567 — **SLEEPING BEAUTY** — ADMIT ONE
5. No: 1234567 — **JACK AND THE BEANSTALK** — ADMIT ONE
6. No: 1234567 — **PINOCCHIO** — ADMIT ONE
7. No: 1234567 — **PUSS IN BOOTS** — ADMIT ONE
8. No: 1234567 — **PETER PAN** — ADMIT ONE

A. A wooden toy with a long nose

B. A crocodile that has swallowed a clock

C. A clever cat

D. Two ugly stepsisters

E. A genie who comes out of a magic lamp

F. A magic bean and a golden egg

G. A sleeping spell and a handsome prince

H. A wicked queen and a magic mirror

Pair Up the Stockings

I just couldn't resist opening my 'lock that doesn't lock' and taking a look at these wonderful Christmas stockings!

There are six pairs – can you match them up?

Santa's Busy Night

Santa Claus works **SO-SO-SO** hard on Christmas Eve to deliver all the presents. I think he deserves a nice, long nap on Christmas Day – don't you? (I'll be having one for sure!)

To find something important that Santa needs on Christmas Eve, put one letter in each of the boxes to make two words. The letter will be the last letter of the first word and also the first letter of the second word, e.g.

```
        BOO  K  ITE

     MIS  [ ]  AME
      OW  [ ]  EG
      PI  [ ]  EL
      SK  [ ]  NK
      EG  [ ]  AP
      AS  [ ]  AT
```

Finish Father Christmas

Wouldn't you love to meet Santa Claus and see his jolly smiling face? Perhaps you already have?

Can you draw Santa? Here's a verse from one of my favourite poems to help you… And don't forget his beard!

> *His eyes – how they twinkled! His dimples, how merry!*
> *His cheeks were like roses, his nose like a cherry!*
> *His droll little mouth was drawn up like a bow,*
> *And the beard of his chin was as white as the snow.*

(from ''Twas the night before Christmas' by Clement Clarke Moore)

Christmas Stocking Scramble

Because I stay in different homes during the holidays, I've watched many children hanging up their stockings on Christmas Eve. They all have one thing in common – they get unsqueakably excited! And so do I!

Can you unscramble the letters to find out what this stocking has inside it?

CLACOOETH
_ _ _ _ _ _ _ _ _

NOXBAPIT
_ _ _ _ _ _ _ _

LABL
_ _ _ _

RAC
_ _ _

LUZEPP
_ _ _ _ _ _

OKOB
_ _ _ _

LOLD
_ _ _ _

NEGORA
_ _ _ _ _ _

Terrific Turkey-doku

I've made up another hamsteriffic Sudoku puzzle for you! It's a little more challenging than the others - so why not use a pencil in case you need to rub it out.

Can you fill in all the empty squares with letters, so that every row (across), column (down) and 2 x 3 box contains the letters **TURKEY**?

T	U				R
K	E		Y		
	T	K	Y	R	
E	Y			K	U
Y		T	E		K
	E	U		T	Y

Match the Crackers

The loud noise of crackers being pulled used to **SCARE-SCARE-SCARE** me! But now I know all about crackers, I'm not scared any more – I'm just excited about what's inside them!

Can you match up all these cracker halves? Draw lines between them.

BANG!

BANG!

BANG!

BANG!

BANG!

BANG!

Humphrey's Jolly Jokes 6

What do you get if you eat the Christmas decorations?

Tinsel-itis.

> I always know when Christmas is coming — I just look at the school calen-deer!

What goes 'Ho, ho, whoosh, ho, ho, whoosh'?

Santa in a revolving door.

Where do ghosts go at Christmas time?

To the phanto-mime.

What's white and goes up?

A confused snowflake.

What did Adam say the day before Christmas?

'It's Christmas, Eve.'

What's on the Sleigh?

I **LOVE-LOVE-LOVE** surprises! And there are just so many at Christmas time.

Santa is bringing surprise gifts for everyone on his sleigh. Can you fill in the missing letters and find out what they are?

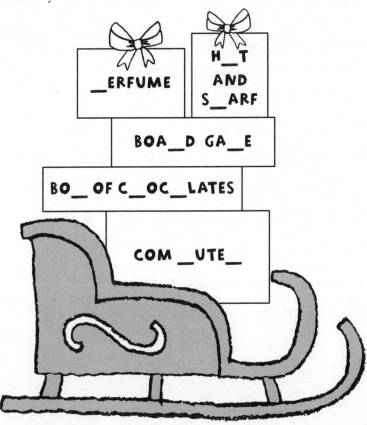

_ERFUME

H__T
AND
S__ARF

BOA__D GA__E

BO__ OF C__OC__LATES

COM __UTE_

Crack the Code

As you know, I'm a hamster that likes to crack secret codes. And I've discovered a hamsteriffic new code. It's more than a hundred years old and is called the Pigpen Code – because of its shape.

Each letter is represented by the shape it is in – see the diagram below. If you use the second letter in the shape, you put a dot into it. Easy!

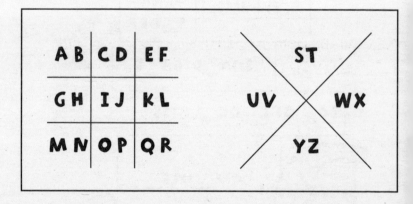

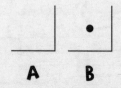

Can you read my Christmas message in Pigpen Code?

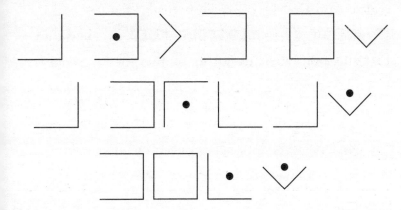

Now will you write me a message in Pigpen Code too?
I can't **WAIT-WAIT-WAIT** to read it!

Humphrey's Chilly Crossword

December can be **COLD-COLD-COLD** – they should call it Decem-brrrr! Even though I've got a fur coat I won't be venturing outside – I like it here in my nice, warm cage.

To while away the long winter evenings, I've been making up a crossword – can you solve it?

DOWN

1. When the sun shines on to a snowman, it starts to _ _ _ _.

2. Watch them falling from the sky – so pretty! And no two are ever alike.

5. When water freezes, it turns to _ _ _.

6. You should put these on your hands if you're going out in the cold.

ACROSS

2. Have you ever walked over ice? Watch out – it's incredibly _ _ _ _ _ _ _ _.

3. A little house made out of ice.

4. A really fun thing for humans to do on an ice rink. But it's easy to slip!

7. On cold days, they say that Jack _ _ _ _ _ has sprinkled an icy white covering over everything.

Odd One Out 2

Take a close look at all these Christmas items.
Can you circle one picture in each set of three that is
the odd one out?

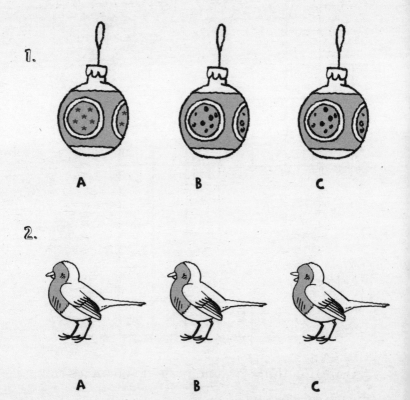

1.

A   B   C

2.

A   B   C

3.

A   B   C

4.

A   B   C

Jumbled Jokes

I **LOVE-LOVE-LOVE** jokes – sometimes they make me squeak so hard I have to lie down for a while!

I've taken six of my favourite Christmas jokes and mixed them up – can you match the jokes with the correct answers?

Answer

1. **What do you get if you cross an apple with a Christmas tree?** ☐

2. **What's red and white and red and white and red and white?** ☐

3. **What's the wettest animal in the world?** ☐

4. **What did one snowman say to the other?** ☐

5. **What does Tarzan sing at Christmas time?** ☐

6. **Why are reindeer such bad dancers?** ☐

A. Jungle bells, jungle bells . . .
B. A rain-deer.
C. They have two left feet!
D. A pineapple.
E. Ice to meet you!
F. Santa Claus rolling down a hill.

Letter to Santa

Have you ever written a letter to Santa Claus? I wrote a tiny note one year and left it just outside my cage on Christmas Eve. In the morning it was gone – and my Christmas wish came **TRUE-TRUE-TRUE**! (But I can't tell you what it was, because it was secret!)

Why don't you fill in this letter to Santa and tell him your Christmas wish?

Dear Santa

I hope you and your _____ are well.

My name is _____ and I am _____ years old.

I am a boy/a girl/a hamster.

This year I have been very good/quite good/ sometimes good, sometimes not so good/not very good.

There's something else I need to tell you about me!

_____

_____

My Christmas wish is _____

_____

_____

_____

Thanks, Santa!

Humphrey's Christmas Message

Wishing you all a furry happy Christmas and a paw-sitively wonderful New Year!

JOY-JOY-JOY TO THE WHOLE WIDE WORLD! (And that includes YOU!)

Answers

p. 7 **Santa's Sack** JIGSAW.

p. 8-9 **Festive Word Grid** 1. CANDLES 2. PAPER 3. TURKEY
4. HOLLY 5. LOG Vertical word: **CAROL.**

p. 11 **Christmas Wordsearch**

S	E	H	G	L	O	R	A	C
A	C	G	A	I	K	I	H	R
N	K	A	M	C	H	T	R	A
T	S	O	E	L	N	I	A	C
A	O	H	S	E	L	L	N	K
C	K	V	V	P	E	S	A	E
L	S	D	I	S	A	E	N	R
A	A	R	N	L	B	R	W	C
U	N	I	G	B	A	V	T	G
S	T	N	E	S	E	R	P	Y

p. 12 **Humphrey Sings** 1. Night 2. Manger 3. First 4. Twelve 5. Angels
6. Halls 7. King 8. Town.

p. 14-15 **Aldo's Christmas Ladder** 1. BIKE 2. MIKE 3. MILE 4.
MILK 5. SILK 6. SICK 7. LICK 8. LOCK 9. SOCK.

p. 17 **Festive Sudoku 1**

p. 18-19 **Santa Around the World** 1. China 2. Egypt 3. Peru 4. India 5. Italy 6. Canada.

p. 23 **Snowy True or False?** 1. True. 2. False. All snowflakes are completely different! 3. True 4. True 5. True 6. True 7. False. A severe snowstorm is called a blizzard. 8. False. Snow is actually colourless. It only looks white because it reflects sunlight!

p. 25 **Snowman Spot-the-difference** B.

p. 26-27 **Humphrey's Secret Christmas Code** Santa Claus is coming to town.

P	R	A	N	C	E	R	N	C
A	C	G	A	I	U	I	H	R
R	E	N	N	O	D	P	R	A
B	S	H	E	L	N	I	I	T
L	D	H	P	E	L	N	E	D
I	K	A	V	L	E	M	A	A
T	S	D	N	M	O	E	N	S
Z	A	R	F	C	B	D	W	H
E	N	O	G	B	E	V	U	E
N	E	X	I	V	E	R	P	R

p. 30-31 **Tasty Wordsnake**

P	U	N	D	A	M
D	D	A	Y	E	R
I	N	C	O	G	C
P	G	T	R	N	I
I	E	U	A	N	F
A	C	O	R	G	F
K	E	S	P	E	U
U	T	E	C	S	T
R	Y	G	U	A	S
K	E	R	A	V	Y

p. 34-35 **Snowflake Sorting** C and H are the same.

p. 36 **Nativity Wordsearch**

B	A	B	Y	J	E	S	U	S
E	C	E	L	B	A	T	S	R
T	E	N	Y	O	D	A	R	A
H	S	H	E	L	R	R	I	W
L	D	H	P	E	L	N	E	I
E	K	O	G	L	E	M	A	S
H	S	N	N	M	O	X	N	E
E	A	R	F	K	B	D	W	M
M	N	O	G	B	E	G	U	E
Q	E	X	F	V	E	Y	P	N

p. 37 **Festive Sudoku 2**

p. 38-39 Rockin' Rhymes 1. Treat 2. Day 3. Snow 4. Sack 5. Night 6. There.

p. 40-41 Odd One Out 1. A 2. B 3. C 4. B.

p. 44-45 Santa's Wordsnake

S	A	S	E	E	E
T	N	E	N	R	T
A	W	R	T	O	W
R	O	P	S	N	S
K	C	K	L	L	L
S	A	I	E	E	B
H	S	G	H	E	Y
O	P	E	R	N	M
D	N	I	L	F	I
E	E	R	E	C	H

p. 46 Reindeer True or False? 1. True 2. True 3. False. Females have antlers too! 4. True 5. True 6. False. A reindeer can run faster than a human. 7. True 8. False. Rudolph had a very shiny nose!

p. 47 Humphrey Sings 2 1. White 2. Winter 3. Child 4. Rudolph 5. Frosty 6. Merry 7. Santa Claus 8. Jingle.

p. 50 Festive Food Mince Pie, Yule Log, Plum Pudding, Roast Potato, Chestnut Stuffing, Brussel Sprout, Cranberry Sauce.

p. 51 Humphrey's Tasty Treat Gingerbread.

p. 52 Humphrey's Tasty Treat We found a lot of words: motel, smile, mile, slime, totem, lime, smelt, melt, mole, elm, toilet, most, meet, moist, omit, slim, mitts, item, mist, some, most, stem, seem, time, steel, sleet, stile, stilt, stole, soil, title, eel, oil, lest, list, else, lots, slot, lies, lose, lost, sole, isle, tilt, tie, test, sit, set, toe, to, is, it, so. How many did you find?

p. 54-55 Humphrey's Secret Christmas Code 2 How many days left until Christmas?

p. 56 Humphrey's Christmas List Bubble bath, tie, broom, book, diary, whistle, piano.

p. 58-59 Rockin' Rhymes 2 Mouse, head, sleigh, glows, jolly, hoof, bright, king.

p. 60 What's in the Tree? ROBIN.

p. 61 Christmas Tree Maze

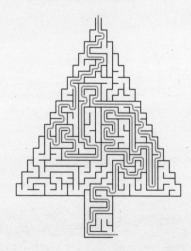

p. 62-63 **Christmas Picture Crossword**

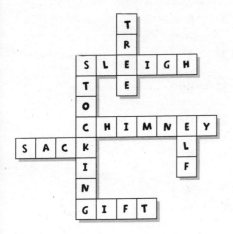

p. 64-65 **Panto Puzzler** 1. E 2. D 3. H 4. G 5. F 6. A 7. C 8. B.

p. 68 **Santa's Busy Night**

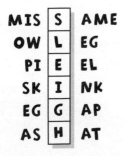

p. 70 **Christmas Stocking Scramble** Chocolate, paintbox, ball, car, puzzle, book, doll, orange.

p. 71 **Terrific Turkey-doku**

T	U	Y	K	E	R
R	K	E	U	Y	T
U	T	K	Y	R	E
E	Y	R	T	K	U
Y	R	T	E	U	K
K	E	U	R	T	Y

p. 75 **What's on the Sleigh?** Perfume, hat and scarf, board game, box of chocolates, computer.

p. 76-77 **Crack the Code** A hug is a great gift.

p. 78-79 **Humphrey's Chilly Crossword**

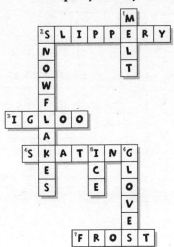

p. 80-81 **Odd One Out 2** 1. A 2. C 3. A 4. B.

p. 82 **Jumbled Jokes** 1. D 2. F. 3. B 4. E 5. A 6. C.